Lottie and Ludo

Lottie woke with a start. She could hear footsteps outside. She jumped up and looked around. Who could it be?

There was a crash, and a small pane of glass in the door smashed.

What was happening? "Ludo, wake up!" she woofed.

"I'm awake," squawked Ludo, above her. "What's going on?" He flapped to the side of his cage and peered at the door.

"I don't know," Lottie whimpered. "But I don't like it."

Jenny Dale's Best Friends

More Best Friends follow soon!

Best♥Friends

Lottie and Ludo

by Jenny Dale
Illustrated by Susan Hellard

A Working Partners Book

MACMILLAN CHILDREN'S BOOKS

Special thanks to Liss Norton

First published 2003 by Macmillan Children's Books Ltd
a division of Macmillan Publishers Limited
20 New Wharf Road, London N1 9RR
Basingstoke and Oxford
www.panmacmillan.com

Associated companies throughout the world

Created by Working Partners Limited
London W6 0QT

ISBN 0 330 40079 7

1 3 5 7 9 8 6 4 2

A CIP catalogue record for this book is available from
the British Library.

Typeset by SX Composing DTP, Rayleigh, Essex
Printed and bound in Great Britain by Mackays of Chatham plc, Kent

Chapter one

"Yippee!" woofed Lottie, the little brown puppy. "Here comes Miss Miller!" She ran to the front of her pen, wagging her tail so hard that her body wriggled. She could see Miss Miller through the glass in the front door. It was breakfast time!

Miss Miller came into the rescue centre. She was a tall, smiling lady with grey curly hair. "Good morning, Lottie," she said, opening the door of Lottie's pen.

Lottie scampered out and rolled over

so that Miss Miller could stroke her
tummy. Then she scrambled to her paws
and looked up at the cockatiel that lived
in the cage above her pen. "Come on,
Ludo," she barked. "Let's play while
Miss Miller gets our breakfast."

Ludo stretched his beautiful long
wings. "Coming," he squawked. He flew
over to the cage door, gripped the bolt in
his beak and slid it back. The door
opened and Ludo flew out.

"Well done, Ludo!" said Miss Miller.
"Who's a clever boy then?"

Ludo flew on to Miss Miller's shoulder
and gently nibbled her ear.

Miss Miller stroked his feathers.
"Who's a clever boy then?" she said
again.

Ludo didn't say anything.

Lottie watched Ludo with her head on one side. She couldn't understand why he never talked to Miss Miller. "Let's play hide-and-seek," she woofed.

Ludo loved playing hide-and-seek. He flew off Miss Miller's shoulder and on to the desk by the door. "Off you go, then," he squawked, tucking his head under his wing.

Lottie bounded down the long passage between the pens. "Morning!" she barked as she passed Tibs and Tinker, the tabby kittens. "Wake up!" she woofed to the sleepy rabbits.

She reached the guinea-pigs' hutch at the end of the passage. It was raised up on short legs. Lottie crouched as low as she could and squeezed underneath. "Don't tell Ludo I'm here," she woofed softly.

"All right," squeaked Ginger, the biggest guinea pig.

The rabbits in the hutch next door hopped up to the wire and stared at Lottie, twitching their noses.

Ludo listened to Lottie's paws padding on the floor as she scampered along the passage. At last the padding stopped. Lottie must have found a hiding place, Ludo thought. "Coming, ready or not!" he squawked. He stretched his wings and flapped up to the ceiling, so that he could look all round the rescue centre. He couldn't see a puppy anywhere. Lottie was very good at hiding.

With his sharp eyes, Ludo noticed that the rabbits were all staring into the guinea-pigs' hutch. "What are you looking at?" he asked. But all he could see were the guinea-pigs dozing in the straw.

Suddenly he spotted something moving underneath the hutch. He swooped down. It was Lottie's tail, wagging madly as usual!

"Found you!" Ludo squawked in delight.

Lottie came out, looking very excited. "It's your turn to hide now," she barked. She shut her eyes and listened to the swish of feathers as Ludo flew away.

I know a good hiding place, Ludo thought as he landed at the door of Lottie's pen. He hopped inside and crouched behind her basket. She'll never think of looking for me here.

After a few moments, Lottie opened her eyes and began to search. She ran to Miss Miller's desk and looked under it. Ludo wasn't there. He wasn't on the shelves above the desk, either.

"Where are you?" Lottie called.

Ludo kept very still.

"Breakfast time, Lottie," said Miss Miller, coming down the passage. She put Lottie's bowl inside her pen.

"Yummy!" Lottie woofed. Playing hide-and-seek always made her hungry. She would look for Ludo afterwards. She dashed into her pen. There was something sticking out from behind her basket. It was a feathery tail! She crept up and pounced. "Found you!" she barked.

Ludo jumped when he felt soft puppy paws grabbing his tail. He came out from behind the basket. "I thought I'd picked a really good hiding place," he squawked.

"It *was*," Lottie woofed. "I only came into my pen to eat my breakfast."

Ludo flapped up to his cage. He hoped Miss Miller had given him plenty of sunflower seeds. They were his favourite.

Lottie was just about to tuck into her breakfast when she heard footsteps outside. She looked through the glass door and saw a pair of legs approaching, wearing blue trousers.

There was a knock at the door.

"Hello," said Miss Miller. "Who's at the door?"

Mr Ross, the postman, came in. Lottie liked him. He had a parcel under his arm. "Sorry I'm late," he said. "My alarm clock didn't go off." He took some letters out of his bag and gave them to Miss Miller.

"Thank you," she said.

"This parcel's for you, too," Mr Ross told her, handing it over.

"Oh, lovely!" cried Miss Miller. She tore open the parcel. There was a long string of small, brightly coloured flags inside. "It's the bunting for the Open

Day tomorrow," Miss Miller explained. "It will make the garden look very colourful."

Ludo watched Miss Miller unwrap the bunting. He decided to play a trick. He flew down, grabbed the end of the string with his claws and flapped away with it. Coloured flags trailed out behind him.

When he reached the far end of the rescue centre, he perched on a pen and looked back, feeling very pleased with himself. All the pens along the passage were draped with flags.

"Bad boy!" scolded Miss Miller.

Mr Ross laughed.

Dropping the string of flags, Ludo flew on to Miss Miller's shoulder and rubbed his head on her neck. He knew she wasn't really cross.

"Bad boy," Miss Miller laughed, stroking his head. "Come on, Ludo, why don't you say something? Bad boy. Bad boy."

Lottie stopped eating to watch Ludo. She'd heard that some birds could speak person language. She wondered why

Ludo never wanted to try.

"Bad boy," Miss Miller said again.

Ludo kept his beak shut tight. He had an important reason for not talking in person language. His friend Perkin, a large blue-and-green parrot, had been good at talking and a family had taken him home to live with them. But Ludo loved living in the rescue centre; he didn't want to leave.

"I hope you'll be coming to our Open Day tomorrow, Mr Ross," said Miss Miller, while they picked up the bunting. "There'll be cakes to buy, a raffle and lots of games."

Lottie pricked up her ears and looked at Ludo. Cakes and games! That sounded fun.

Ludo put his head on one side and listened to Miss Miller too.

"And everyone will be able to meet the animals," Miss Miller continued. She smiled round at her animals. "Perhaps some of you will find new homes."

Lottie began to feel very excited. Scrap and Dodger, who lived at the centre, had told her that dogs were meant to have families of their own. Lottie liked living in the rescue centre with her best friend Ludo, but sometimes she thought it might be nice to have her own family. They'd be able to do all the things that Scrap and Dodger had talked about, like playing ball and going for long walks. She didn't want to leave Ludo, but maybe he would find a family too.

Ludo's wings drooped. His tummy felt
as though it was full of butterflies. At
least nobody will want me if I don't
speak person language, he thought.
I'll just have to make sure that I don't
say a word.

chapter Two

Lottie woke early the next morning. "Wake up, Ludo! It's the Open Day today!" she barked.

She heard a flutter of wings above her. Ludo was unlocking his cage. A moment later he flew down to Lottie's pen.

"I couldn't sleep," he squawked. "I keep thinking about the Open Day." He was feeling a bit better about it today because he was looking forward to visiting the cake stall and seeing all the coloured flags.

Miss Miller came into the rescue centre with Gemma and Rachel, who helped to look after the animals. "Please would you brush the rabbits, Gemma?" she said. "And could you help to set up the stalls, Rachel?"

Lottie scampered to the front of her pen. She watched Gemma fetch a brush and go to the rabbits' cage. "I hope she brushes me, too," Lottie woofed, looking down at her soft fur. "I want to look smart today."

"I don't need to be brushed," squawked Ludo. "I can preen my own feathers." And he stroked his glossy wing with his beak.

Gemma came to brush Lottie straight after breakfast. Lottie tried to keep still but she couldn't stop her tail from wagging. The brush felt tickly as it smoothed her fur and it made Lottie wriggle. Gemma then tied a big red bow loosely around Lottie's neck.

Lottie felt very proud of her shiny coat and red bow. "Look at me, Ludo!" she woofed. The cockatiel was sitting on top of her pen, nibbling a sunflower seed.

He peered over the edge to look at her.

"You look great!" squawked Ludo.

"Can you see what's happening outside?" Lottie asked.

Ludo flew over to the desk. "There's a big crowd by the gate," he told Lottie. "And Miss Miller's letting them in." He flapped back to the top of Lottie's pen.

Lottie heard voices outside, then a boy in a red shirt came into the rescue centre with his mum and dad. He ran along the passageway and crouched down by Tibs and Tinker's pen. "Look, Mum! Kittens! Can I stroke them?" he asked.

Gemma opened the pen and lifted out the kittens. The boy hugged Tinker, with his face pressed against the kitten's soft grey fur. Lottie could hear Tinker purring. "I hope someone will stroke me," she woofed. She stayed at the front of her pen where everyone would see her.

Ludo looked outside. A man was walking across the grass. He seemed familiar, but Ludo couldn't work out why. He had a little girl with him. She had long fair hair. Suddenly Ludo recognized him. "It's Mr Ross!" he squawked. "He isn't wearing his blue trousers today."

Lottie pushed her nose through the bars as Mr Ross came in. She was sure he would stroke her. "Mr Ross! I'm over here!" she barked.

"Look at that lovely puppy, Daddy!" said the little girl.

"Oh, that's Lottie," said Mr Ross. He led the little girl over to Lottie's pen.

The girl knelt down to stroke Lottie. Lottie licked her hand and the girl giggled. "Isn't she sweet?" she said.

"Yes, she is," agreed Mr Ross. He bent down and ruffled Lottie's ears.

Ludo caught Mr Ross's sleeve with his beak and tugged it.

"Hello, Ludo," said Mr Ross. He stroked Ludo's feathers. "I hope you're not going to fly away with any flags today," he laughed.

Ludo let go of Mr Ross's sleeve and hopped from foot to foot. Perhaps he'd be able to think of some different tricks to play. But he wasn't going to talk in person language, that was for sure.

Miss Miller came over. "Would you like to take Lottie for a walk around the garden, Kirsty?" she asked the little girl.

"Yes, please!" said Kirsty, jumping up.

Yippee! thought Lottie. She liked Kirsty already, and she wanted to see what was going on in the garden now all the visitors were here.

Miss Miller unlocked Lottie's pen and

the puppy scampered out with a tiny bark of excitement. She wriggled impatiently while Miss Miller put on her collar and lead. "Here you are," said Miss Miller as she handed the lead to Kirsty.

"Come on, Lottie," said Kirsty, patting her.

"Are you coming too, Ludo?" Lottie woofed as Kirsty led her towards the door.

Ludo thought for a moment. He really wanted to have a look at the stalls in the garden but he was still a bit worried. What if someone decided to take him home? Maybe he should stay inside. "You go, Lottie," he squawked. "I'll stay in here."

Chapter Three

Lottie looked around the garden in amazement. She'd never seen so many people. Everywhere she looked there were legs. She wished Ludo could see too. Miss Miller must be very pleased to have so many visitors.

"Let's go to the duck pond," said Kirsty.

Lottie looked up at her, puzzled. There weren't any ducks here! She followed Kirsty and Mr Ross over to a bright blue paddling pool. It was surrounded by people holding long, thin fishing rods. Lottie squeezed past them to look into the pool. It was full of bright yellow plastic . . . ducks! Oh, they aren't real ducks, Lottie thought. The people with the fishing rods were trying to pick up the ducks by the little hooks on their heads.

Mr Ross handed Kirsty a fishing rod. She dropped Lottie's lead as she took it but Lottie didn't run off. She liked being with the little girl. Kirsty tried to hook a duck but they kept bobbing away from her to the other side of the paddling pool. Lottie felt very sorry for her. She wondered if there was anything she could do to help.

*

24

Back in the rescue centre, Ludo was beginning to feel bored. He looked through the open door. He could see Lottie's tail wagging madly among a crowd of people. It seemed a shame to miss out on the fun. Normally, they did everything together. Ludo decided to go and join his friend. He flew out of the door, swooped across the garden and landed in a tree behind Lottie. She was watching some yellow ducks. Ludo could see that Kirsty was having trouble picking one up with her rod. It looked very tricky. Ludo had a much better idea.

"Why don't you help her, Lottie?" he squawked.

Lottie looked round in surprise. Ludo

was perched in a tree just behind her.

"You could catch one of those ducks easily," he pointed out.

"You're right, I could," Lottie barked. "Thanks, Ludo. That's a great idea!" She took a deep breath and jumped right into the pool.

SPLASH!

The little yellow ducks bounced all over the place. Lottie grabbed one in her mouth.

"Oh, Lottie!" Kirsty cried. "Dogs aren't meant to catch the ducks."

Lottie scrambled out of the pool and dropped the duck. Her ears drooped. She hoped Kirsty wouldn't be cross with her.

But she saw that Kirsty was laughing.

"Don't worry, Lottie. Come on, Dad. Let's go and buy a cake before Lottie catches any more ducks for us."

"Cakes? Yummy!" Lottie barked in delight. She gave herself a good shake, spraying water everywhere.

Ludo flapped away quickly. He hated getting wet! He spotted Miss Miller in the crowd and flew on to her shoulder.

"What a beautiful bird!" said a man. "Can he talk?"

"No. I've tried to teach him, but he's never said a word," Miss Miller replied, smoothing Ludo's feathers.

"What a shame!" the man said.

Phew, thought Ludo. My plan's working. He put his head on one side and watched Lottie and Kirsty squeeze

through the crowd towards the cake
stall.

While Kirsty was choosing a cake,
Lottie stuck her nose under the
tablecloth and sniffed around. There
were lots of yummy crumbs!

Suddenly Lottie spotted an extra big
crumb on the other side of the table.
She stretched towards it. Lottie felt the
lead slip out of Kirsty's hand but it
didn't matter. She'd go straight back to
her.

Two men were standing close to the
crumb. One was a tall, thin man
wearing black boots. The other man was
short and fat.

As Lottie licked up the crumb, she
heard the men talking.

"They must have made loads of money today," said the short man.

"Yeah," agreed the tall man. "I wonder where they keep it?"

"I saw a desk near the door of the rescue centre," said the first man. "Maybe they keep it in there."

Lottie was puzzled. Why were the men

talking about money in Miss Miller's desk?

The tall man laughed. "That will make it easy to get our hands on!"

Lottie padded over and sniffed at the tall man's black boots.

"Get away, you stupid mutt," the man said angrily. He twitched his foot, as if he wanted to kick Lottie.

Lottie backed away under the table. The men didn't seem to like animals at all! So why had they come to the Open Day? She decided to ask Ludo later on. Lottie pushed her way out from under the tablecloth and looked for Kirsty.

"There you are! I thought I'd lost you," Kirsty said, picking up the end of Lottie's lead. "Let's go to the toy stall."

Lottie wagged her tail. She was glad to be going away from those unfriendly men. The toy stall sounded like much more fun!

"The Open Day was brilliant!" woofed Lottie, that evening. Ludo was in his cage on top of her pen.

"Tibs and Tinker were really excited when they found out they were going home with that boy," Lottie continued. "I wonder if I'll get a new home too." She scratched her ear.

Ludo wasn't really listening. He was sorting out the food in his bowl, pushing all the sunflower seeds to one side. They were his favourite and he always saved them until last. He thought about going to a new home and shivered. What if his new owners never gave him sunflower seeds?

"I'm going to sleep now, Lottie," he said. "All that flying around the garden has worn me out."

Lottie yawned and stretched. Then she climbed into her basket and snuggled

down. Her eyes closed. "Goodnight, Ludo," she woofed sleepily.

But Ludo stayed awake for a long time. He really hoped no one came back to take him home.

Chapter Four

Lottie woke with a start. She could hear footsteps outside. She jumped up and looked around. It was just beginning to get light. For a moment she thought it was Mr Ross delivering letters. Then she heard voices. It didn't sound like Mr Ross. Who could it be?

There was a crash, and a small pane of glass in the door smashed.

Lottie's heart started pounding with fear. What was happening? "Ludo, wake up!" she woofed.

"I'm awake," squawked Ludo, above her. "What's going on?" He flapped to the side of his cage and peered at the door.

"I don't know," Lottie whimpered. "But I don't like it."

A hand wearing a thick, black glove reached through the broken glass and unlocked the door. Two men came into the rescue centre.

Lottie's fur stood on end. They were the unfriendly men who'd been talking by the cake stall.

"I told you this would be easy," said the short, fat man. The broken glass crunched under his feet. "It shouldn't take long to find the money and get away before the old lady wakes up."

36

"Oh, Lottie, what are we going to do?"
Ludo squawked.

"We've got to wake Miss Miller!"
woofed Lottie. She began to bark as
loudly as she could. "Help, help! Miss
Miller, there are some nasty men in the
rescue centre!"

Nobody came.

"Oi!" growled the tall man. "Stop
making that noise!"

"Don't worry," said the other man.
"Dogs are always barking in here."

Lottie stopped barking. Her ears
drooped. It was true. She often barked
just because she was happy. So did Scrap
and Dodger. Miss Miller wouldn't take
any notice.

The tall man yanked open the drawers

in Miss Miller's desk and rummaged through them, spilling papers everywhere.

Suddenly he stopped. Tucked beneath a pile of papers at the back of the bottom drawer, he spotted a tin. "This feels heavy," he said as he lifted it out. He put the tin on the desk and opened it. "Look at this!" he yelled. "We're rich!" He took out a handful of money and stuffed it into his bag.

"That must be the Open Day money!" Ludo squawked. "Oh Lottie, these men are robbers!"

Suddenly Lottie heard a van draw up outside. The two men didn't seem to notice. They were too busy cramming money into their bag.

"That sounds like Mr Ross's van,"
Lottie woofed. "We've got to let him
know what's happening before the
robbers escape."

"You'll have to bark again," Ludo told
her.

"What's the point?" Lottie woofed
sadly. "He won't know that there's

anything wrong if he hears me barking. I bark all the time." Suddenly she had an idea. "You'll have to tell him what's going on, Ludo!"

"Me? I'm always squawking. He won't take any notice of me, either," Ludo replied.

"He will if you use *person* language," Lottie woofed, her tail wagging with excitement.

"Person language?" echoed Ludo. "But I can't!"

"I'm sure you could if you tried," Lottie urged. "Miss Miller's been teaching you for ages!"

Ludo hopped from foot to foot. This was terrible! How could he make Lottie understand? "But I don't *want* to speak person language," he squawked. "If I do, someone will want to take me home, just like they did with Perkin."

Lottie stared up at him in surprise. "Don't you want a new home?"

"No! I want to stay here with Miss Miller."

"That's the lot then," said the short man, zipping up the bag. "Let's get out of here."

"Ludo, there's no time to worry about that now," Lottie barked. "We've got to stop them getting away with Miss Miller's money! Please speak to Mr Ross."

Ludo thought for a moment. He loved Miss Miller so much, he couldn't bear it if all her money was stolen.

"All right, I'll try," he squawked. "But what if I can't do it?" he asked.

"Of course you can," Lottie barked, hoping she was right. He had to! It was their only hope.

Ludo shut his eyes. He took a deep breath, then opened his beak very wide . . .

chapter five

"HELLO! WHO'S AT THE DOOR?
BAD BOY! OH DEAR!" Ludo shouted.

"What was that?" cried one of the
men. He whirled round, dropping the
bag of money. Coins clattered to the
floor. Some of them rolled into Lottie's
pen.

Ludo stared at Lottie in amazement.
"I did it! I spoke person language!"

"Well done!" woofed Lottie. "Keep
going!"

"BAD BOY!" Ludo shrieked again.

This was fun! "WHO'S AT THE DOOR?"

"There's someone in here!" yelled the tall man. He looked round fearfully.

The short man dropped to his knees and began to gather up the money. "Give me a hand, Bert," he said, stuffing money into his pockets.

The tall man noticed the coins in Lottie's pen. "Look at all these. We can't leave them here." He unlocked the door.

Lottie saw her chance. She charged out as soon as the door opened. She grabbed the robber's trouser leg with her teeth and held on tight.

"Get off me, you stupid mutt!" the man bellowed, trying to shake Lottie off. But she gritted her teeth and clung on.

Ludo unbolted his cage and flew out as fast as he could. He had to help Lottie! He pecked the tall man on the nose. "Bad boy!" he squawked.

"Ow!" yelled the man. He stumbled backwards and fell over.

"Bad boy!" Ludo screeched again. He flew round and round the man's head, while Lottie kept hold of his trouser leg so he couldn't get up. The robber held his head in his hands and groaned.

The short man had finished picking up the money. He leaped up and ran towards the door.

Oh no! Lottie thought. He's going to get away with Miss Miller's money!

Suddenly the door burst open and Mr Ross raced into the rescue centre. "Stop right there!" he shouted, grabbing the robber with both hands.

Lottie wanted to bark for joy but she didn't want to let go of the man's trouser leg. Instead she wagged her tail. They had caught the robbers!

Just then, Miss Miller ran in, wearing her dressing gown and slippers. "I've called the police!" she said. "They'll be here any second."

She turned to Mr Ross. "I heard noises," she explained. "I'm so grateful that you were here to catch them."

"That's OK," said Mr Ross. He was still hanging on to the struggling robber. "But it's Lottie and Ludo you should be thanking, not me."

Miss Miller looked at the best friends

in surprise. "Well done, you two," she said proudly.

Lottie still had hold of the tall man's trouser leg. Ludo was flapping in circles around his head. This robber wasn't going to escape!

"How did you know the robbers were in here?" Miss Miller asked Mr Ross.

"I heard someone shouting," he said.

"Shouting?" echoed Miss Miller. She looked at the two robbers. "Why were you shouting?"

"It wasn't us," the short man said sulkily. He glared at Ludo. "It was that stupid bird."

Ludo flapped his wings crossly. Stupid? He'd saved Miss Miller's money!

Suddenly Lottie heard a wailing sound outside. She pricked up her ears.

"Here come the police," said Mr Ross.

The robbers looked at each other and groaned. "We'd have got away if it hadn't been for those stupid animals," they complained.

Three policemen raced in. They put handcuffs on the robbers, then searched their bag and pockets. "This belongs to you," the police sergeant said to Miss Miller. He handed her the stolen money.

"Thank you," said Miss Miller. She put the money back in the tin. "I'll pay it into the bank this morning."

As two of the policemen led the robbers to the police car outside, Miss Miller and Mr Ross told the sergeant what had happened. "They were caught by Lottie and Ludo?" he said. "Well I never did!"

Miss Miller bent down to stroke Lottie. "Well done, Lottie."

Ludo flew down on to Miss Miller's shoulder. "And well done, Ludo," Miss Miller said, smoothing his feathers.

"Clever boy!" squawked Ludo. "Well done, Lottie! Well done, Ludo!"

"Oh, Ludo! You *are* a clever boy!" exclaimed Miss Miller, looking delighted. "I always knew you could talk."

Lottie froze. Ludo had spoken person language! She looked at the sergeant. Would he want to take Ludo home now he knew he could talk?

Ludo shut his eyes tight and pressed himself against Miss Miller's neck. How could he have been so silly?

The sergeant laughed. "That bird would be very useful to us down at the police station."

Ludo opened one eye and stared at him in horror. This was just what he'd

51

been afraid of. He was going to be sent
to a new home and he'd never see Lottie
or Miss Miller again!

chapter Six

"Oh, Ludo," Lottie whined, gazing up at the parrot. Her ears drooped. It looked like Ludo had been right all along. She was going to lose her best friend.

Ludo clung to Miss Miller's shoulder, his wings sagging. Was she going to make him leave straight away?

Miss Miller reached up and stroked Ludo's feathers. Then she shook her head. "I'm sorry," she said to the sergeant. "But Ludo lives here with me.

I couldn't let him go, I'm afraid. Not to anyone."

Ludo twisted his head round and stared at Miss Miller. She wasn't going to send him away after all! He danced up and down on her shoulder.

"Hooray!" he squawked. "I can stay!"

"That's brilliant!" Lottie woofed,

jumping up and running madly in circles. "It didn't matter that you spoke person language after all!"

"Well it's a shame we can't have him," said the policeman. "He'd have made a great watchdog – or bird!"

Miss Miller laughed. "Thank you so much for your help," she said.

As the policemen drove the robbers away in their police car, Mr Ross bent down to stroke Lottie. "What a brave little dog you are," he said, ruffling her ears. Lottie wriggled happily.

"Time for breakfast," said Miss Miller. "I think Ludo deserves some extra sunflower seeds today, and I've got a bone in the fridge which will be just right for Lottie."

Sunflower seeds? Bones? Lottie and
Ludo looked at each other in delight.
They should catch robbers *every* day!

Lottie and Ludo were playing chase up
and down the passageway that afternoon
when the door opened and Mr Ross and
Kirsty came in with Miss Miller. They
were all beaming.

"It's Kirsty!" Lottie barked. She
danced round Kirsty's legs, wagging her
tail madly.

"Hello, Lottie," said Kirsty. "Guess
what? Daddy said you can come home
and live with me!" She bent down and
hugged the puppy.

Lottie gave a bark of happiness, then
licked Kirsty's face. She was going to live

with Kirsty and Mr Ross! They'd be able
to go out for walks and play lots of
games.

"Lottie will love living with you," said
Miss Miller. "But we'll miss her."

Then Lottie thought about Ludo. He
was her best friend. She would really
miss him. She looked around for him.

Ludo was sitting on the edge of Miss Miller's desk. His head and wings drooped. "I'll miss you, Lottie," he squawked, sadly.

"I'll miss you, too," Lottie woofed. She looked from Ludo to Kirsty and back again. If only there was a way she could stay with both of them.

"Don't worry, Miss Miller, I'll bring Lottie with me on my rounds," said Mr Ross. "So you'll be able to see her every day."

"Did you hear that, Ludo?" woofed Lottie. "We'll still get to see each other!"

"Every day!" Ludo squawked, hopping up and down on Miss Miller's desk. "We'll be able to play hide-and-seek and chase. And catch robbers, if there are any about!" He flew down and nibbled Lottie's ear. Lottie licked his feathers.

Miss Miller fetched Lottie's bowls and basket and gave them to Mr Ross.

Kirsty clipped on Lottie's lead. "Come on, Lottie," she said. "Let's go home."

Lottie looked back at Ludo as she trotted towards the door by Kirsty's side. Everything had turned out perfectly! She'd got a family of her very own but she would still see Ludo and Miss Miller. And Ludo didn't have to leave the rescue centre, ever.

"See you tomorrow, Ludo," she woofed happily.

"Bye, Lottie," squawked Ludo cheerfully, flying on to Miss Miller's shoulder. "See you tomorrow."